EXPOSED! MORE MYTHS ABOUT AMERICAN HISTORY

COWBOYS DIDN'T ALWAYS WEAR HATS

EXPOSING MYTHS ABOUT THE WILD WEST

Fitchburg Public Library
5530 Lacy Road
Fitchburg, WI 53711

BY JILL KEPPELER

Gareth Stevens
PUBLISHING

Please visit our website, www.garethstevens.com. For a free color catalog of all our high-quality books, call toll free 1-800-542-2595 or fax 1-877-542-2596.

Library of Congress Cataloging-in-Publication Data

Names: Keppeler, Jill.
Title: Cowboys didn't always wear hats : exposing myths about the wild west / Jill Keppeler.
Other titles: Exposing myths about the wild west
Description: New York : Gareth Stevens Publishing, [2020] | Series: Exposed! More myths about American history | Includes index.
Identifiers: LCCN 2018045300| ISBN 9781538237465 (pbk.) | ISBN 9781538237489 (library bound) | ISBN 9781538237472 (6 pack)
Subjects: LCSH: Cowboys–Juvenile literature. | Frontier and pioneer life–West (U.S.)–Juvenile literature.
Classification: LCC F596 .K44 2020 | DDC 978–dc23
LC record available at https://lccn.loc.gov/2018045300

First Edition

Published in 2020 by
Gareth Stevens Publishing
111 East 14th Street, Suite 349
New York, NY 10003

Copyright © 2020 Gareth Stevens Publishing

Designer: Sarah Liddell
Editor: Therese Shea

Photo credits: Cover, p. 1 Montanabw/Wikimedia Commons; background texture used throughout IS MODE/Shutterstock.com; ripped newspaper used throughout STILLFX/Shutterstock.com; photo corners used throughout Carolyn Franks/Shutterstock.com; p. 5 outdoorsman/Shutterstock.com; p. 7 (top) Charles Marian Russell/Adam Cuerden/Wikimedia Commons; p. 7 (bottom) Hohum/Wikimedia Commons; p. 9 (top) Pictorial Parade/Staff/Archive Photos/Getty Images; p. 9 (bottom) Killiondude/Wikimedia Commons; p. 11 (main) Scewing/Wikimedia Commons; p. 11 (inset) Andrew J. Jurbiko/Wikimedia Commons; p. 13 JPHiggs/Wikimedia Commons; p. 15 (main) Transcendental Graphics/Contributor/Archive Photos/Getty Images; p. 15 (inset) Charles Marion Russell/Godot13/Wikimedia Commons; p. 17 Sean Pavone/Shutterstock.com; p. 19 (main) Everett Historical/Shutterstock.com; p. 19 (inset) George Sheldon/Shutterstock.com; pp. 21 (left), 27 (inset) Bettmann/Contributor/Bettmann/Getty Images; p. 21 (right) Fototeca Storica Nazionale./Contributor/Hulton Archive/Getty Images; p. 23 (top) Joseph Sohm/Shutterstock.com; p. 23 (map) Armita/Shutterstock.com; p. 25 eAlisa/Shutterstock.com; p. 27 (main) Silver Screen Collection/Contributor/Moviepix/Getty Images; p. 29 De Agostini/Biblioteca Ambrosiana/De Agostini PIcture Library/Getty Images.

All rights reserved. No part of this book may be reproduced in any form without permission in writing from the publisher, except by a reviewer.

Printed in the United States of America

CPSIA compliance information: Batch #CS19GS: For further information contact Gareth Stevens, New York, New York at 1-800-542-2595.

CONTENTS

Tales of the Wild West 4
The Cowboy Way 6
Women in the West 10
Wild or Mild? 12
Wild Bill 18
The Kid 20
Express to the West 22
The Red Ghost 24
The West in Movies 26
More to the Stories 28
Glossary 30
For More Information 31
Index 32

Words in the glossary appear in **bold** type the first time they are used in the text.

TALES OF THE WILD WEST

Everyone has heard stories of gunfights, cowboys, **outlaws**, and lawmen in the American Wild West. People and events of this exciting time are featured in countless books, movies, TV shows, and even games.

But how true are these stories? Do they match what happened in real life? While many tales of the West have hints of the truth, many more are based in **fiction**. The Wild West was a perfect subject for storytellers, and some of their tales became **myths** over time.

The time of the Wild West (also called the Old West) is about 1865 to 1895. By the beginning of 1896, most of the territories that were part of the West had become states.

THE COWBOY WAY

THE MYTH: COWBOYS WERE ALWAYS WHITE MEN.

THE FACTS:

When many picture the Wild West, they think of a cowboy riding his horse, gun in hand, on the lookout for outlaws and Indians. The cowboy is usually white.

In real life, cowboys were a **diverse** group. They were white, Native American, black, or Mexican. In fact, the first cowboys were Mexicans who called themselves vaqueros. That comes from the Spanish word for "cow"—vaca.

GIDDYUP!

So, what *is* a cowboy? Real cowboys take care of and drive herds of cattle. It's not an easy life—far harder than the movies show it to be!

VAQUERO

Another name for a cowboy is a "buckaroo." This word comes from the word vaquero.

THE MYTH: COWBOYS WERE TOUGH OLDER MEN WHO WORE A KIND OF HAT THAT WE CALL A COWBOY HAT TODAY.

THE FACTS:

In the Old West, cowboys were often quite young. Many were malnourished, which means they were sickly because they didn't get enough of the right things to eat. It was hard to stay healthy on a long cattle drive!

Cowboys also didn't often wear Stetson hats, the kind we know today as a cowboy hat. They wore other kinds of hats, though, including bowler hats.

NOT-SO-CLEAN COWBOYS?

Real cowboys were often quite dirty and stinky. They didn't bathe much—or brush their teeth!

Bat Masterson, a famous lawman of the Wild West, is shown in the top picture in a bowler hat. Cowboys sometimes wore this kind of hat. Others wore flat-topped hats.

WOMEN IN THE WEST

THE MYTH: THE WILD WEST WAS NO PLACE FOR A WOMAN.

THE FACTS:

White women had some opportunities in the West that they didn't have elsewhere. In 1869, the Wyoming Territory gave women the right to vote. It was the first US state or territory to do this.

Several other western states and territories gave women the right to vote before the **19th Amendment** was passed in 1920. However, women of other races, including African American, Asian, and Native American, had few freedoms.

LANDOWNERS

Women had a greater chance of owning land in the West than in the East, especially closer to the Mexican border.

Some famous Wild West women took on unusual roles for their time. Annie Oakley was a sharpshooter in "Buffalo Bill" Cody's Wild West Show. At right, she uses a mirror to shoot behind her!

WILD OR MILD?

THE MYTH: THE WILD WEST WAS, WELL, WILD! IT WAS A **VIOLENT** PLACE.

THE FACTS:

There were dangers in the Old West, but many historians don't think it was as lawless as stories and movies show.

For example, some people believe bank robberies happened there all the time. In fact, there were only eight bank robberies in about 40 years across 15 western states and territories. Towns were small then. Banks were close to the **sheriff's** office. That was a little too close to jail for some outlaws!

Butch Cassidy and other outlaws robbed a bank in Telluride, Colorado, in 1889, stealing about $20,000. That's over $500,000 in today's money!

THE REAL STORY

Native Americans weren't the danger to whites as some stories tell. The Oregon Trail was a route, or path, that more than 250,000 settlers followed west in the 1800s. Only about 1 to 4 percent of deaths on the trail were caused by native attacks.

THE MYTH: THERE WAS NO GUN CONTROL IN THE WILD WEST.

THE FACTS:

While guns were widely used on the **frontier**, they weren't nearly as uncontrolled as people often believe.

By the later 1800s, even the wildest towns of the Wild West—such as Tombstone, Arizona, and Dodge City, Kansas—had laws stopping people from carrying guns inside town limits. Leaders wanted people to move there, and that wouldn't happen if the towns weren't thought to be safe.

CHECK YOUR GUN

Visitors to some Wild West towns had to leave their guns at the sheriff's office or another safe place while they were there.

Popular books of the time showed the Wild West as a place full of shootouts and excitement. Many people believed these stories over the truth.

THE MYTH: THERE WERE OFTEN GUNFIGHTS AND SHOOTOUTS AT HIGH NOON IN WILD WEST TOWNS.

THE FACTS:

Shootouts in the Old West didn't happen often at all! There were a few famous ones that really did occur, such as the shootout at the O.K. Corral in 1881.

However, gunfights at high noon, or exactly noon, are mostly a work of fiction. Writers put these fights in stories (and later in movies and TV shows) to make events seem more exciting.

AT THE O.K. CORRAL

The O.K. Corral was in Tombstone, Arizona. The shootout actually took place in a lot behind the corral, or livestock pen. The Earp brothers (Wyatt, Virgil, and Morgan) and Doc Holliday took on an outlaw gang—and won.

Today, you can see actors recreate the famous gunfight near O.K. Corral in Tombstone, Arizona.

WILD BILL

THE MYTH: "WILD BILL" HICKOK WAS THE BEST GUNFIGHTER IN THE WILD WEST.

THE FACTS:

Many of the tales about Wild Bill are true. He was an excellent shot and led an exciting life. However, he was a popular subject of Old West stories. Many of the true stories became **exaggerated** as people retold them.

Hickok himself exaggerated some of the events of his life. He once claimed to have killed 100 men. He probably killed only six or seven!

DEAD MAN'S HAND

Hickok was killed during a card game in Deadwood, South Dakota, in 1876. A story says he was holding a pair of black aces and a pair of black eights. This is now called a "dead man's hand."

Wild Bill's name was really James Butler Hickok. He was a sheriff, army scout—and some say a Civil War spy! There's no proof of this, however.

THE KID

THE MYTH: BILLY THE KID WAS THE DEADLIEST WILD WEST OUTLAW.

THE FACTS:

The Kid's real name was probably Henry McCarty. He sometimes went by William Bonney Jr. Much of his life is mixed with myth. He was shot dead when he was 21.

One tale said he killed a man for each year of his life. However, he probably killed fewer than 10. He also didn't kill a man just for snoring too loud like one story said—though another outlaw did!

PAT GARRETT

REWARD
($5,000.00)

Reward for the capture, dead or alive, of one Wm. Wright, better known as

"BILLY THE KID"

Age, 18. Height, 5 feet, 3 inches. Weight, 125 lbs. Light hair, blue eyes and even features. He is the leader of the worst band of desperadoes the Territory has ever had to deal with. The above reward will be paid for his capture or positive proof of his death.

JIM DALTON, Sheriff.

DEAD OR ALIVE!
"BILLY THE KID"

Many people wrote books about Billy the Kid. One of the most famous was written by Pat Garrett—the sheriff who killed him.

EXPRESS TO THE WEST

THE MYTH: RIDERS FOR THE PONY EXPRESS DELIVERED ALL THE MAIL IN THE WILD WEST.

THE FACTS:

The Pony Express did deliver mail to the West. On horseback, they could travel much faster across the frontier than a **stagecoach** could. However, the Pony Express lasted only about 18 months! Riders made fewer than 400 runs, and the business lost a lot of money.

This way of delivering the mail died out when the **telegraph** connected the West to the rest of the country.

MAP OF THE PONY EXPRESS

The Pony Express lasted from April 1860 to October 1861. It ran between Missouri and California.

THE RED GHOST

THE MYTH: A RED CREATURE WAS THE TERROR OF ARIZONA. IT WAS 30 FEET (9.1 M) TALL AND KILLED PEOPLE!

THE FACTS:

When people started seeing an odd reddish creature in the Arizona territory in the 1880s, stories of its deadly nature quickly spread. It was named the "Red Ghost." Some said it could disappear right in front of their eyes!

Surprisingly, there's a bit of truth to this weird tale, though the creature wasn't nearly as spooky or dangerous as some thought. The Red Ghost was most likely just a fast wild camel!

ARMY CAMELS

The US military brought camels from Europe and Africa to the West to carry gear and do other jobs. By 1857, there were about 75 camels in all.

Because camels don't need much water and are used to desert conditions, the US military thought they'd be useful in the West. However, many were turned loose at the start of the American Civil War (1861–1865).

THE WEST IN MOVIES

THE MYTH: MOST STORIES OF THE WILD WEST WERE CREATED DURING THE 1800s.

THE FACTS:

It's true that many tales of the Wild West were created back then. However, many more were told years later by American film companies.

From the 1920s to the 1950s, Hollywood made popular cowboy movies based in the Wild West called Westerns. As the years passed, Westerns began to show different points of view about life back then, including the point of view of Native Americans.

THE GREAT TRAIN ROBBERY

The first **narrative** movie was *The Great Train Robbery*, which came out in 1903. This 10-minute movie was set in the Wild West but was mostly filmed on the East Coast.

JOHN WAYNE

GENE AUTRY

Gene Autry, the "Singing Cowboy," and John Wayne were two of the most famous movie cowboys.

MORE TO THE STORIES

The Wild West was a key place and time in US history, and many Americans still love to watch and read stories about it. However, these tales are often one-sided and can't be considered history.

For example, many of the "heroes" of the West killed Native Americans over land. But the Native Americans had lived there long before settlers arrived. White Americans "won" the West at great cost to native peoples. Learn more about the Wild West so you can continue to separate fact from fiction!

Native Americans are often shown as being the enemies of white settlers in movies. In real life, they were forced from their homes and their way of life.

29

GLOSSARY

19th Amendment: the addition to the US Constitution, the highest law in the nation, that gave women the right to vote in 1920

diverse: differing from one another

exaggerate: to think of or describe something as larger or greater than it really is

fiction: a made-up story

frontier: a part of a country that has been newly opened for settlement

myth: an idea or story that is believed by many people but that is not true

narrative: having the form of a story

outlaw: a person who has broken the law and who is hiding or running away to avoid punishment

sheriff: an elected official who is in charge of enforcing the law in a county or town

stagecoach: a large carriage pulled by horses that was used in the past to carry passengers and mail along a route

telegraph: a method of communicating using electric signals sent through wires

violent: having to do with the use of force to harm someone

FOR MORE INFORMATION

Books

Pascal, Janet B. *What Was the Wild West?* New York, NY: Grosset & Dunlap, 2017.

Rice, Dona Herweck. *Bad Guys and Gals of the Wild West.* Huntington Beach, CA: Teacher Created Materials, 2017.

Sheinkin, Steve. *Which Way to the Wild West? Everything Your Schoolbooks Didn't Tell You About Western Expansion.* New York, NY: Roaring Book Press, 2015.

Websites

American West: Cowboys
www.ducksters.com/history/westward_expansion/cowboys.php
Find information on the daily life of a cowboy here.

10 Things You Didn't Know About the Old West
www.history.com/news/10-things-you-didnt-know-about-the-old-west
The History Channel presents a collection of unusual facts about the Wild West.

Publisher's note to educators and parents: Our editors have carefully reviewed these websites to ensure that they are suitable for students. Many websites change frequently, however, and we cannot guarantee that a site's future contents will continue to meet our high standards of quality and educational value. Be advised that students should be closely supervised whenever they access the internet.

INDEX

19th Amendment 10
Autry, Gene 27
Billy the Kid 20, 21
Buffalo Bill Cody's Wild West Show 11
Cassidy, Butch 13
cowboys 6, 7, 8, 9, 27
dead man's hand 19
Dodge City, Kansas 14
Earp brothers (Wyatt, Virgil, and Morgan) 17
Garrett, Pat 21
Great Train Robbery, The 27
Hickok, James Butler "Wild Bill" 18, 19
Holliday, Doc 17
Masterson, Bat 9
Native Americans 6, 10, 13, 26, 28
Oakley, Annie 11
O.K. Corral 16, 17
Oregon Trail 13
Pony Express 22, 23
Red Ghost 24, 25
Stetson hats 8
Tombstone, Arizona 14, 17
Wayne, John 27
women 10, 11